Before I go to sleep

This book belongs to

....

....

Written by Ronne Randall
Illustrated by Tony Kerins

This edition published by Parragon in 2011

Parragon
Queen Street House
4 Queen Street
Bath BA1 1HE, UK

Copyright © Parragon Books Ltd 2008

ISBN 978-1-4454-5411-5

Printed in China

Before I go to sleep

PaRRagon

Bath • New York • Singapore • Hong Kong • Cologne • Delhi
Melbourne • Amsterdam • Johannesburg • Auckland • Shenzhen

Before I go to sleep,
Mummy brings my drink,
and kisses me
night-night.

Night-night,
Mummy.

Daddy reads me a story
about the little red sailboat.

Then he kisses me
night-night.

Night-night,
Daddy.

Where's Waggy dog?

There you are.
Night-night, Waggy dog.

Before I go to sleep,
I kiss Teddy night-night.

Night-night, Teddy.
Are you sleepy yet?

Kitty isn't sleepy yet.

I wonder where
she goes at night?

Before I go to sleep,

I'll snuggle down

and close my eyes.

Where is Teddy going?
Teddy and Waggy dog
are following Kitty.
Wait for me, I'll come too.

We'll sail away in our

little red sailboat

over Grandma and Grandpa's house

and across the pond to say,

Night-night, ducks. Night-night, sky.

Night-night, moon.

Night-night, stars.

Night-night, world.

Teddy, are you sleepy yet?
We're almost home, now.

Night-night, me.

Night-night, you.

Night-night, everyone.

Sweet dreams.